The Happy Lion

THE

by Louise Fatio

McGRAW-HILL BOOK COMPANY

NEW YORK   TORONTO   LONDON

HAPPY LION

pictures by Roger Duvoisin

Also by Louise Fatio and illustrated by Roger Duvoisin
THE HAPPY LION AND THE BEAR
THE HAPPY LION IN AFRICA
THE HAPPY LION'S QUEST
THE HAPPY LION ROARS
THE THREE HAPPY LIONS
A DOLL FOR MARIE
RED BANTAM

Tenth Printing

There was once a very happy lion.

His home was not the hot and dangerous plains of Africa
where hunters lie in wait with their guns,
it was a lovely French town with brown tile roofs and gray shutters.
The happy lion had a house in the town zoo, all for himself,
with a large rock garden surrounded by a moat,
in the middle of a park with flower beds and a bandstand.

Early every morning,
François, the keeper's son, stopped on his way to school
to say, *"Bonjour*, Happy Lion."

Afternoons,
Monsieur Dupont, the schoolmaster, stopped on his way home
to say, *"Bonjour,* Happy Lion."
Evenings,
Madame Pinson, who knitted all day on the bench by the bandstand,
never left without saying, *"Au revoir,* Happy Lion."

On summer Sundays,
the town band filed into the bandstand to play waltzes and polkas.
And the happy lion closed his eyes to listen. He loved music.
Everyone was his friend and came to say *"Bonjour"*
and offer meat and other tidbits.

He *was* a happy lion.

One morning,
the happy lion found that his keeper
had forgotten to close the door of his house.
"Hmm," he said, "I don't like that. Anyone may walk in."
"Oh well," he added on second thought,
"maybe I will walk out myself and see my friends in town.
It will be nice to return their visits."

So the happy lion walked out into the park
and said, "*Bonjour*, my friends" to the busy sparrows.
"*Bonjour*, Happy Lion," answered the busy sparrows.
And he said, "*Bonjour*, my friend" to the quick red squirrel
who sat on his tail and bit into a walnut.
"*Bonjour*, Happy Lion," said the red squirrel, hardly looking up.

Then the happy lion went into the cobblestone street
where he met Monsieur Dupont just around the corner.
"Bonjour," he said, nodding in his polite lion way.
"Hooooooooohhh . . ." answered Monsieur Dupont,
and fainted onto the sidewalk.
"What a silly way to say *bonjour*," said the happy lion,
and he padded along on his big soft paws.

"Bonjour, Mesdames," the happy lion said farther down the street
when he saw three ladies he had known at the zoo.
"Huuuuuuuuuuuuuhhhhhh . . . " cried the three ladies,
and ran away as if an ogre were after them.
"I can't think," said the happy lion, "what makes them do that.
They are always so polite at the zoo."

"*Bonjour*, Madame." The happy lion nodded again
when he caught up with Madame Pinson near the grocery store.
"Oo la la . . . !" cried Madame Pinson,

and threw her shopping bag full of vegetables into the lion's face.

"A-a-a-a-choooooo," sneezed the lion.

"People in this town are foolish, as I begin to see."

Now the lion
began to hear the joyous sounds of a military march.
He turned around the next corner,
and there was the town band, marching down the street
between two lines of people.
Ratatatum ratata ratatatum ratatata boom boom.

Before the lion could even nod and say, "*Bonjour*,"
the music became screams and yells.
What a hubbub!
Musicians and spectators tumbled into one another
in their flight toward doorways and sidewalk cafes.
Soon the street was empty and silent.

The lion sat down and meditated.
"I suppose," he said, "this must be the way people behave
when they are not at the zoo."
Then he got up

and went on with his stroll in search of a friend
who would not faint, or scream, or run away.
But the only people he saw were pointing at him excitedly
from the highest windows and balconies.

Now what was this new noise the lion heard?

"Toootoooooot . . . hoootoooooootooooot . . ." went that noise.

"Hooooot toooooooTOOOOOOOOOOHHHOOOOT . . ." and it grew

more and more noisy.
"It may be the wind," said the lion.
"Unless it is the monkeys from the zoo,
all of them taking a stroll."

All of a sudden
a big red fire engine burst out of a side street,
and came to a stop not too, too far from the lion.
Then a big van came backing up on the other side of him
with its back door wide open.

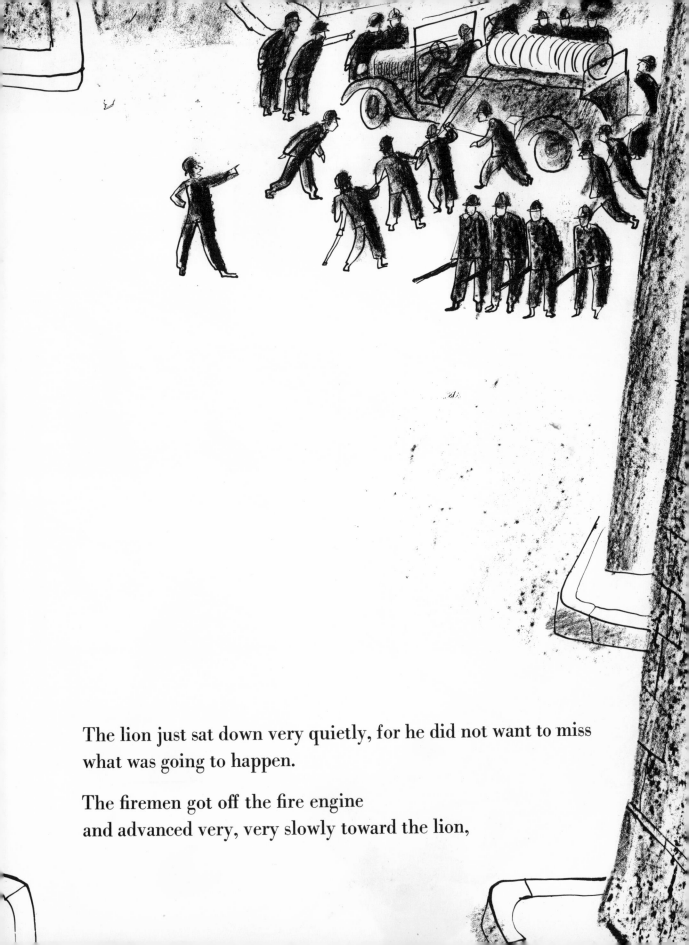

The lion just sat down very quietly, for he did not want to miss
what was going to happen.

The firemen got off the fire engine
and advanced very, very slowly toward the lion,

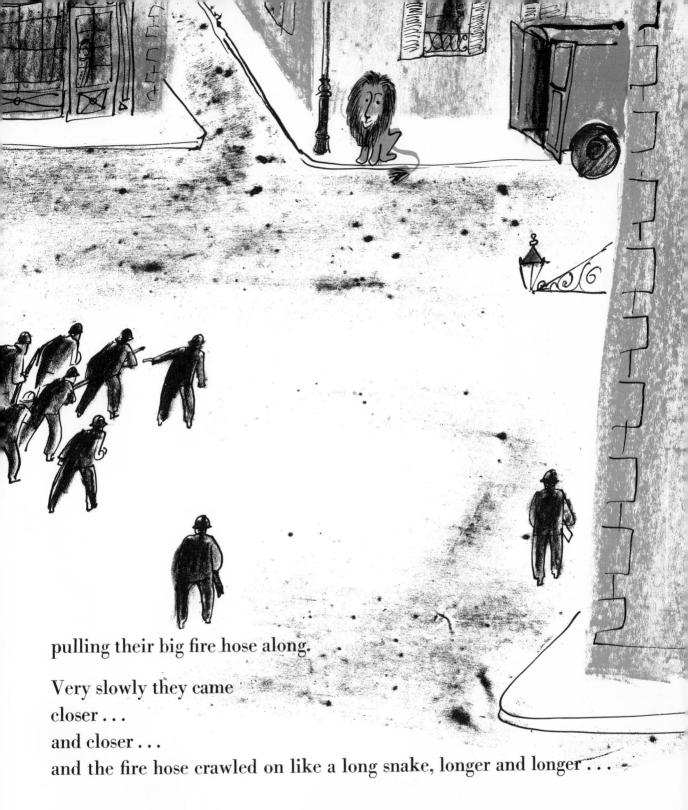

pulling their big fire hose along.

Very slowly they came
closer . . .
and closer . . .
and the fire hose crawled on like a long snake, longer and longer . . .

SUDDENLY,
behind the lion,

a little voice cried, "*Bonjour*, Happy Lion."
It was François, the keeper's son, on his way home from school!
He had seen the lion and had come running to him.
The happy lion was so VERY HAPPY
to meet a friend who did not run and who said "*Bonjour*"
that he forgot all about the firemen.

And he never found out what they were going to do, because
François put his hand on the lion's great mane and said,
"Let's walk back to the park together."
"Yes, let's," purred the happy lion.

So François and the happy lion walked back to the zoo.
The firemen followed behind in the fire engine,

and the people on the balconies and in the high windows
shouted at last, "BONJOUR! HAPPY LION!"

From then on
the happy lion got the best tidbits the town saved for him.
But if you opened his door
he would not wish to go out visiting again.
He was happier to sit in his rock garden
while on the other side of the moat
Monsieur Dupont, Madame Pinson,
and all his old friends came again
like polite and sensible people
to say *"Bonjour*, Happy Lion."
But he was happiest
when he saw François walk through the park
every afternoon on his way home from school.
Then he swished his tail for joy,
for François remained always his dearest friend.